S0-BQZ-393

READ ALL OF THESE

NATE THE GREAT

DETECTIVE STORIES

BY MARJORIE WEINMAN SHARMAT

WITH ILLUSTRATIONS BY MARC SIMONT:

Nate The Great
and The
Pillowcase

by Marjorie Weinman Sharmat
and Rosalind Weinman

illustrations by Marc Simont

DELACORTE PRESS/NEW YORK

Delacorte Press

Published by Delacorte Press
Bantam Doubleday Dell Publishing Group, Inc.
1540 Broadway, New York, New York 10036

Library of Congress Cataloging in Publication Data

Sharmat, Marjorie Weinman.
    Nate the Great and the pillowcase/by Marjorie Weinman Sharmat and Rosalind Weinman; illustrations by Marc Simont.
        p.   cm.
    Summary: Nate the Great investigates the disappearance of a homemade pillowcase belonging to Rosamond's cat Big Hex.
    ISBN 0-385-31051-X
    [1. Mystery and detective stories.]   I. Weinman, Rosalind.
II. Simont, Marc, ill. III. Title.
PZ7.S5299Navd   1993
[E]—dc20   JAN 2   1994   92-34405
                                                                  CIP
                                                                  AC
Manufactured in the United States of America
October 1993
10 9 8 7 6 5 4 3 2 1
WOR

For our wonderful mother and father,
Anna and Nathan Weinman

With love,
M. W. S. and R. W.

I, Nate the Great, am a sleepy detective.

My dog Sludge is a sleepy dog.

We have just finished a sleepy case.

It started a few hours ago.

It was two o'clock in the morning.

I was not busy.

I was sleeping.

Sludge was sleeping.

Suddenly the telephone rang.

It woke us up.
Who could be calling me
in the middle of the night?
"Hello," I yawned.
It was Rosamond.
"A pillowcase is missing," she said.
"Can you help me find it?"
"No," I said, and I hung up.
The telephone rang again.
I answered it.

"Sleep on another pillowcase,"
I said.

"It's not my pillowcase,"
Rosamond said.

"It belongs to Big Hex."

"Your cat has a pillowcase?"

"Of course," Rosamond said.

I yawned. "You want me to get up
from my sleep to look for
a cat's pillowcase?"

"Yes. I thought that

Big Hex could sleep without it.
But he keeps pacing
up and down,
up and down,
up and down. . . ."
"Doesn't he have a pillow to sleep on?"
"Of course. That's why he
needs the pillowcase."
Rosamond was strange in the daytime.
But she was even more strange
at night. I knew that she
would not let me sleep.
"I will take your pillowcase case,"
I said.
I put on my bathrobe and slippers.
I wrote a note to my mother.

Dear Mother,
I know you are asleep.
I wish I were.
I am looking for a pillowcase
insted of sleeping on one.
I will be back.
Love, Nate The Great

Sludge and I went out into the night.
It was damp, dark, dreary, and shivery.
We hurried to Rosamond's house.
Rosamond looked sleepy and strange,
but not in that order.
Her four cats were there.
Plain Hex, Little Hex, and
Super Hex were asleep.

Big Hex was pacing up and down.
I said, "What does his pillowcase
look like?"
"It's beautiful," Rosamond said.
"I made it myself.
I made four of them.
One for each cat.
All the same.
White with holes around the
open end, and a pretty ribbon
through the holes. See?"
Rosamond pointed to her
sleeping cats.
"Big Hex's pillowcase looks
exactly like theirs?" I asked.
"Oh, no. Big Hex likes to
play with his case.

So now it's slashed and shredded.
I keep washing it.
So it's also shrunken and shriveled.
And he chewed up the ribbon.
So that's gone."
"Let me get this straight.
The missing pillowcase is
slashed and shredded,
shrunken and shriveled.
And it has holes around one end.
And you want it *back*?"
Rosamond smiled.

"Yes, Big Hex just loves it."
"When was the last time you saw it?"
"This afternoon.
I washed all my cats' things.
I had four laundry bags full.
One for each cat.
I even washed the bags.
Then I hung everything out to dry."
"Did you hang four pillowcases?"
"Of course," Rosamond said.
"One for each cat.
Then Annie came over with Fang.
I told her this was
my big laundry day for pets.
So we undressed Fang,
and I washed his sweater

and neck bandanna.
Then I hung them out to dry."
"Then what?"
"When everything was dry,
I put it all in my laundry basket."
"Were the four pillowcases there?"
"Yes."
"Then what?"
"I brought the basket into the house

and dumped everything on my bed.
Then Annie and I tried
to dress Fang in his nice clean clothes.
Well, that's the last time I'll ever try
to dress that dog!"

"What happened?"

"Fang growled at me. He showed every
one of his teeth. I ran out of the room.
Then I yelled to Annie
to take Fang's clothes home,
and to take Fang with them.
And that's what she did."

"Did you go back to your laundry
after that?"

"No. My cats were hungry,
so I fed them.
Then I read to my cats."

"You read to your cats?"
"Fifteen minutes each day."
"When did you get back to
your laundry?"
"Just before I went to bed.
I looked for the night things.

The pillowcases and nightshirts.
That's when I found out
that Big Hex's pillowcase was missing.
And one of Little Hex's nightshirts."
"You are missing the pillowcase *and*
a nightshirt?"
"No. I know where the nightshirt is.
Annie took it by mistake. I think she
just grabbed stuff in her arms
when she left."
"Aha! Perhaps Annie took Big Hex's
pillowcase by mistake."
"No," Rosamond said. "I called her
before I called you."
"You woke her, too?"
"Well, I found out that she has

Little Hex's nightshirt.

But she doesn't have the pillowcase.

See what a good detective I am?"

I, Nate the Great, yawned.

"Since you are such a good detective,

solve this case," I said.

"Sludge and I are going back to sleep."

"Wait," Rosamond said.
"I'm not a *great* detective.
You solve this case."
"Perhaps your pillowcase is
still in this room,
or you lost it
between the clothesline
and this room.
Sludge and I will look."
Sludge and I looked inside.
And outside. No luck.

I said, "Tell me,
has anyone else been in this room?"
"Only Annie and Fang and my cats."
"Very well. I must go to
Annie's house.
Call her and tell her
I'm coming."
Sludge and I went out into the night.
It was colder than before.
I wrapped my bathrobe tighter around me.
I flashed my flashlight on the ground.

Perhaps Annie had taken the
pillowcase and did not know it.
Perhaps she had dropped it
between Rosamond's house
and her own house.
But I did not see it.
Annie was waiting inside her house.
Fang was waiting, too. He was wearing
pajamas and a nightcap.
Fang had more clothes than I did.
Fang yawned. His teeth had never
looked bigger.
Annie said, "I know why you're here.
But I don't have the pillowcase.
Here is what happened.
Fang and I went over
to Rosamond's house.

Fang was wearing his neck bandanna
and the sweater I got him
for his birthday.
Fang looked very snazzy.
But after Rosamond washed
and dried his clothes,

Fang didn't want to wear them.
He growled at Rosamond.
She ran out of the room.
I stuffed Fang's clothes
into a laundry bag,
and we left fast."
"Aha," I said. "You were in a hurry."
"Yes. I even took Little Hex's
nightshirt by mistake.
I found it when Rosamond
called me up.
I looked in Rosamond's laundry bag.
I saw Fang's sweater and bandanna
and Little Hex's nightshirt.
Tomorrow I'm going to give back
the nightshirt and the laundry bag."
"Could you also have grabbed

Big Hex's pillowcase by mistake?"
Annie shrugged. "I don't know.
But it's not in the laundry bag now."
"Did you stop anywhere
on the way home?"
"Yes, at Uncle Ned's Day and Night Diner
to get some bones for Fang.

They save him some of their leftovers."
"Aha! Something could have dropped
out of the laundry bag
at the diner,
or between Rosamond's house
and the diner,
or between the diner
and your house.
What streets did you take
to and from the diner?"
"I went the shortest way.
Fang led me.
All the dogs know the shortest way."

Sludge wagged his tail.
He liked the diner.
I thanked Annie for her help.
Then Sludge and I walked out
into the night.
It seemed colder and darker.
"To the diner," I said to Sludge.

Sludge led the way.
I flashed my flashlight.
I did not see the pillowcase.
Sludge and I went inside.
The man behind the counter
looked down at Sludge.
He said, "Every dog in town
must have been in here today.
But lucky you,
I have a big bone left."
Sludge was a happy dog.
I saw pancakes on the menu.
I was an unhappy detective.
I had no money.
But I spoke up.
"I am Nate the Great.
Ned knows me.

I would like five pancakes
and some clues.
I will pay you tomorrow.
Right now I am looking
for a cat's pillowcase."
The man smiled and turned away.
He started to make the pancakes.

I saw a white cloth sticking
out of his back pocket.
Hmmm.
I peered over the counter
to take a closer look.
But the man grabbed the cloth
and wiped the counter with it.
The cloth was small and shredded, and
it had plenty of holes.
Was this the pillowcase?

Was the case solved?
The man put a plate of pancakes
in front of me.
I ate and thought.
Annie must have taken the pillowcase
by mistake and stuffed it
into the laundry bag.
When she stopped at the diner,
the pillowcase fell out.
After Annie and Fang left,

the man saw the pillowcase
and thought it was a rag.
I, Nate the Great, had to be sure.
I had to get that rag!
The man stuffed it back
into his pocket.
Then he bent over.
So did I, Nate the Great.
I reached for the rag.

I pulled it out of his pocket.
I spread it out.
I tried to open it up.
It wouldn't open.
It was not a pillowcase.
It was just a rag.
I stuffed it back
into the man's pocket.
It was time to leave.
But Sludge had not finished
his bone.
"Do you have a doggie bag?" I asked.
The man handed me a bag.
I put the bone
in the bag.
"You can finish your bone at home,"
I said to Sludge.

Sludge and I went out into the night.
"Now we must walk the streets
between the diner and
Rosamond's house,"
I said. "Lead the way."
Sludge and I walked and walked.
I did not see the pillowcase.
I saw newspapers being delivered.
I heard the clinking of milk bottles.
I saw the sun coming up.
"The moon is going down
and the sun is coming up,
and I still have not
solved this case," I said.
Sludge was sniffing the doggie bag.
Suddenly he put his teeth into it.

C–R–U–N–C–H!!!

He ripped the bag and grabbed the bone.

Was Sludge hungry,

or was he trying to tell me something?

Where was the pillowcase?

We could not find it

at Rosamond's house.

It was not in the laundry bag

that Annie took home.

We could not find it
on the streets
or in the diner.
Perhaps there was something
Rosamond and Annie had not told me.
But they had told me
the same story about
what had happened
at Rosamond's house.
Except . . . for one small thing!
Suddenly I knew that
Rosamond and Annie
had both been wrong.
"Come!" I said to Sludge.
Sludge and I rushed back
to Annie's house.

It was hard to do.
My bed slippers were wearing out.
Annie was still awake.
I was glad about that.
Fang was fast asleep.
I was glad about that, too.
"I, Nate the Great, know
where the pillowcase is," I said.

"*You* have it."

"No, I don't," Annie said.

"It is not in the laundry bag."

"I, Nate the Great, say

that is because

it *is* the laundry bag!

You were in a hurry

when you left Rosamond's house.

You grabbed what you thought
was a laundry bag."
"Well, it looked like one,"
Annie said. "It was open
on one end, and it
had holes around the end.
Except the rope was missing
from the holes."

"The holes were for a ribbon,"
I said. "But that does not matter.
Please show it to me."
Annie ran out of the room.
She came back holding up
something white, slashed,
shredded, shrunken, and shriveled.
And full of holes at one end.
"That is Big Hex's pillowcase," I said.
"I was so busy thinking about
the things you carried from
Rosamond's house
that I did not think about
what you carried them *in*.
When Sludge went after his bone
inside a bag tonight,

he only cared about the bone,
not what the bone was in.
Sludge and I were thinking alike."
Sludge wagged his tail.
"We were thinking wrong."
Sludge slunk.
"But how did you *know* that
the laundry bag
wasn't really a laundry bag?"
Annie asked.

I, Nate the Great, smiled.
"Rosamond thought you took
the laundry in your arms.
But you told me that you took it
in a laundry bag.
So why wasn't Rosamond
missing a laundry bag?
Because you never took one!"
Annie was staring at the pillowcase.

"Big Hex sleeps on *this?*" she said.
"It's ugly."
Annie tossed the pillowcase to me.
"My Fang would never
sleep on anything so ugly."
Fang heard his name.
He woke up.
He sniffed the ripped doggie bag.
"Pleasant dreams," I said.

Sludge and I walked to
Rosamond's house.
Slowly.
I now had holes
on the bottoms
of both slippers.
"This case is over," I said
to Sludge. "Now Big Hex can
go to sleep.
You can go to sleep.
I can go to sleep."
I rang Rosamond's doorbell.
I waited.
I rang it again.
I waited.
At last the door opened.
Rosamond was standing there.

Yawning.

"You woke me up!" she said.

"I, Nate the Great, have
solved your case."

I held up the pillowcase.
"Annie took this by mistake.
She thought it was a laundry bag."
Rosamond grabbed the pillowcase.
"Thanks. Big Hex will
get a good night's sleep
tomorrow night."
"What about now?"
"Oh, he got tired of pacing.
He's been sleeping since
you left the house.
Nighty night, Nate."
Rosamond slammed the door.
I, Nate the Great, was mad.
But I was glad that
the case was over.

Sludge and I went home.
We went to bed.
It felt good.
The telephone rang.
I, Nate the Great, answered it.
I knew exactly what to say.
"Wrong number."